MARLOWE DeCHRISTOPHER

GREENCOAT
and the Swanboy

PHILOMEL BOOKS
NEW YORK

Copyright © 1991 by Marlowe deChristopher.
All rights reserved. This book, or parts thereof, may not be reproduced
in any form without permission in writing from the publisher.
This version of the French tale "Greencoat and the Swanboy" originally
appeared in PEEPS INTO FAIRYLAND, published in the late 1890's
by Ernest Nister of London, and reissued in 1986 by Philomel
Books in conjunction with Intervisual Communications, Inc.
Philomel Books, a division of The Putnam & Grosset Book Group,
200 Madison Avenue, New York, NY 10016.
Published simultaneously in Canada.
Printed in Hong Kong by South China Printing Co. (1988) Ltd.
Book design by Nanette Stevenson. The text is set in Goudy Old Style.
Library of Congress Cataloging-in-Publication Data
deChristopher, Marlowe.
Greencoat and the swanboy / illustrated by Marlowe deChristopher. p. cm.
Summary: A swanherd loses his flock but gains a princess in this French fairy tale.
[1. Fairy tales.] 1. Title. PZ8.D29GR 1991 [E]—dc20 89-31946 CIP AC
ISBN 0-399-22165-4
First Impression

For Linda

Green, green rocky road,
Promenade in green.
Tell me who you love,
Tell me who you love.

    – Traditional folk song

Once upon a time there was a swanherd, and his name was Baptiste. One day he was sitting upon the bank of the lake where he kept his flock, and as he sat he played upon a reed pipe he had made for himself, while his swans swam and dived and dabbled, and fed upon the sweet water-grass they loved so well.

Then an old man wearing a strange old green coat came and sat by his side. "That is a pretty tune," he said, "but if you will lend me your pipe I will play you a prettier."

So Baptiste lent the old man his reed pipe, and he played a tune so sweet that Baptiste trembled all over.

"Teach me that tune," cried Baptiste, when he had finished. "Oh! Do please teach me that tune!"

"What will you give me if I do?" asked Greencoat.

"I haven't anything to give you," said the lad sadly. "I am only a poor swanherd."

"Nothing to give?" said Greencoat. "Why, what is that gold band I see around your wrist just under the sleeve of your jerkin? Give me that and you shall learn the tune in five minutes!"

"I can't give you that," said Baptiste, "for it won't come off. It was around my wrist when La Mère Cicotte found me on the step of the village fountain, a babe of a month old, and as I have grown, it has grown. Besides, the priest told me never to part with it for love or money."

"Well, then, lend me your flock of swans," said Greencoat, and his bright sharp eyes twinkled mischievously. "I want them for a night or two."

"Oh! But I can't do that either," cried Baptiste. "The swans are not mine—they are my master's!"

"But I want them!" cried Greencoat, and jumping up, he ran along the edge of the lake, his green coattails fluttering in the breeze. Then he stopped, and putting his fingers in his mouth, he whistled loudly.

And behold, all the swans left off splashing and feeding and diving, and rose with a scream into the air, and circled around and around on their wide white wings.

Then they flew away altogether, through the clear blue sky. And Greencoat vanished!

Baptiste ran and cried in despair at seeing his flock take wing. He whistled, he screamed, he shouted, but it was of no avail.

In less time than it takes to tell it, the flock was a tiny white cloud on the distant horizon.

But Baptiste still ran and ran. He did not dare go back without his swans. What would his master say? On, on he went, over the country-side until at last the night fell and he could see nothing, not even the road under his feet, but still he walked on and on.

Presently he saw lights before him, and as he approached them, he could see it was a great palace. Lights shone from the windows, and crowds of people were thronging inside.

"What is it?" he asked of the porter of the gate. "Is it a festival?"

"It is the Trial of the Golden Band," said the porter. "We are wondering if the Prince will come tonight. But go in and see for yourself. Everyone may go in tonight."

So Baptiste went in with the crowd, across the courtyard, and up
into the Great Hall, where on a dais sat a beautiful maiden in white
robes, and around her were great nobles and ladies splendidly dressed
and glittering with jewels. The hall was full of people, but men-at-
arms kept a passage clear to the dais, and from time to time a gallant
young man in rich costume would go alone up the steps and kneel on
a cushion at the Princess's feet.

Then he would stretch out his right arm and reveal a golden band.
An old gentleman in black velvet, who stood by her side, bent down
and looked at the wristlets. But always, as he did, he shook his head
and then the young man would come back with a dark frown.

"Why does he look so angry?" asked Baptiste of a maiden who stood near.

"Because his wristlet doesn't match hers," answered the girl. "For her father has commanded that only the one who has a wristlet exactly like hers shall be her husband. She is the most beautiful Princess and the richest in all the land, she comes of fairy stock, and they say none but a Fairy Knight can win her." But just at that moment Baptiste caught sight of the old man in the green coat who had whisked away his swans.

"Oh!" cried Baptiste, and he pushed through the crowd and caught the old man by the collar. "So, there you are! What have you done with my swans?"

"Hush!" cried the people around. "You are disturbing the trial!"

"I can't help that!" cried Baptiste and he kept tight hold of the green man. "He stole my swans—I must have my swans!"

"Silence! Silence in the hall!" shouted a herald.

"Oh! But I am not going to be silent!" cried Baptiste. "I must have my swans, for my master trusted them to me!"

"Guards," cried the old man in black velvet. "Guards, what is this tumult? Remove the brawlers!"

"Princess, Princess!" cried Baptiste. "Listen to me, I beseech you. I only ask for justice!"

Then the Princess motioned to Baptiste to approach her, and he, still holding Greencoat by the collar, marched up the passage to the foot of the steps, and all the people stared at him amazedly. For though he was but a poor swanherd, he was taller and fairer to look upon than all the young gallants, and wore his homespun garb with a better grace than they did their silks and velvets. Moreover, as he held Greencoat, his sleeve slipped up, and there on his wrist was a band of gold. "See! See! The wristlet!" cried all the people.

Then the Princess beckoned to Baptiste and he, letting go Green-coat, came to her and put his strong brown wrist by her slender one — and lo, the two wristlets matched exactly, and a little tongue of colored flame darted from one wristlet to another, so that they could scarce draw them apart. Looking at one another, they seemed to have known each other all their lives. "It is the Prince!" said the Princess.

"But he is only a swanherd!" cried the ladies, dismayed.

But the Princess smiled, and made Baptiste stand beside her and all the people hurrahed. Then a sound of music rose outside, and, the great windows being opened, she led Baptiste onto a great balcony.

Lo, on a beautiful lake were all Baptiste's swans, but as he had never seen them before. For some were linked by silver ribbons to shining boats, and in the boats were fairy maidens with gauzy wings, crowned with garlands of flowers, and sprites and fays gamboled and dived and swam, and led the great white birds, where they floated up under the balcony and sang a strange sweet song. And Baptiste knew it quite well, for it was the tune the old man had played on his pipe. Then he heard a queer little laugh, and by his side stood Greencoat!

"Well, Baptiste, here are your swans!" he said. "And are you content with me for borrowing them?"

"Quite content, and I give you thanks into the bargain," he answered, "for if you stole my swans, you gave me this," and Baptiste kissed the Princess's hand.

And so they were married, the Princess and Baptiste, and lived
happily all the rest of their lives.